Ant and Honey Bee
What a Pair!

Megan McDonald

illustrated by G. Brian Karas

WALKER BOOKS
AND SUBSIDIARIES

LONDON · BOSTON · SYDNEY · AUCKLAND

from:
CRICKET
to:
Ant and Honey Bee

First published 2005 by Walker Books Ltd
87 Vauxhall Walk, London SE11 5HJ

2 4 6 8 10 9 7 5 3 1

Text © 2005 Megan McDonald
Illustrations © 2005 G. Brian Karas

The right of Megan McDonald and G. Brian Karas to be identified
as author and illustrator respectively of this work has been asserted
by them in accordance with the Copyright, Designs and Patents Act 1988

This book has been typeset in Usherwood

Printed in Singapore

British Library Cataloguing in Publication Data:
a catalogue record for this book
is available from the British Library

ISBN 1-84428-221-X

www.walkerbooks.co.uk

For Judi Ingram Adkins
M. M.

For Ben and Sam
G. B. K.

Ant was getting antsy. She stared out the window at the grey clouds. Only a few hours left till Cricket's fancy dress party.

"What can we go as?" she asked her
friend Honey Bee.
"Gardeners," said Honey Bee.
"Gardeners! We've been gardeners
for two years in a row," said Ant.
"Gardeners are boring."

"Then be a cabbage, if it will make you happy," said Honey Bee.

"What will you be if I'm a cabbage?" Ant asked.

"I'll be a bee," said Honey Bee.

"But you *are* a bee!" Ant said. "You can't just be you."

"It's good to be yourself," said Honey Bee.

"You can be that any time," said Ant. "I know. Let's go as a pair of something."

"I'll be the pear and you be the stem," said Honey Bee.

"Not that kind of pear!" said Ant. "A two-things-that-go-together kind of pair."

"Then I'll be an anteater," said Honey Bee,
"and you be the ant."

"Too scary!" said Ant.

Ant thought and thought about things
that go together.

She looked in the kitchen. Marmalade
and jam?

She looked in the bathroom. Toilet
paper and toilet?

She looked in the utility room.
"I know!" she said. "Let's be a
washing machine and tumble dryer!"

"A washer and dryer make a good pair,"
said Honey Bee.
"Yippee! No more gardeners!"

Ant and Honey Bee found two boxes
that were just the right size. Ant cut
holes for her legs and a big hole for her
head in one box. Honey Bee cut holes
for her legs and wings, and a big hole
for her head, in the other box.

Then they made knobs and dials. Ant
drew soapsuds down the front of her
washer.

Honey Bee glued fuzzy
cotton balls for fluff on her
dryer. They worked as hard
as two ants in an anthill. They worked as
hard as two bees in a beehive.

said Ant, just like a washer
when it washes clothes.

"**BUZZZZZZ!**" said Honey Bee, just like a dryer when it's finished drying.

"We make a great washer and dryer!" said Ant.

"We make a great pair!" said Honey Bee.

It was time for Cricket's party. When Ant tried
to walk down the front steps, she could hardly
move her legs. When Honey Bee tried to walk
down the pavement, she could not see where
she was going.

"It's hard to walk when you're a washer,"
said Ant.

"It's hard to see when you're a dryer,"
said Honey Bee.

The wind blew Ant and Honey Bee
down the street, where they bumped
into Beetle and Fly.

"Look! Two dice!" said Beetle.

"No, it's a couple of ice cubes!" said Fly.

"Blub! Blub!" said Ant, so everyone would know she was a washer.

"Buzzzzz," said Honey Bee, so everyone would know she was a dryer.

"Hey! Swiss cheese!" called Butterfly.

"Yum! Yum! Are those moth holes?" asked Moth.

"Show them your spin cycle, Ant," said Honey Bee.

"Show them your tumble dry," said Ant.

Ant spun around in circles. "Blub! Blub!"

Honey Bee bounced up and down.

"Buzzzzz!"

They spun and bounced
all the way down the hill,
where they ran into the Spiders.

"Look! It's an oven and a dishwasher!"
said Old Man Spider.

"No, dear," said Mrs Spider.
"Can't you see – it's two computers."

"Dancing computers. Very
clever!" said Old Man Spider.

"No one knows *what* we are," said
Honey Bee.

"Mr and Mrs Spider thought we were
clever," said Ant.

"No. They thought dancing computers
were clever," said Honey Bee.

Just then, a gust of wind blew over.
Then, *plip.*

Plip.

Plip,

plip,

PLIP!

"Oh, no! Rain!" cried Ant. "Run!"

"We can't run," said Honey Bee. "We
can hardly walk!"

Ant and Honey Bee waddled through the pouring rain, all the way to Cricket's party.

"My washer is leaking!"
said Ant.

"My dryer is all wet!"
said Honey Bee.

Ant and Honey Bee did not look like a washer and dryer. They did not even look like dice or ice cubes or computers. They did not look like a two-things-that-go-together pair.

They looked like soggy blobs of wet cardboard. A couple of mud pies.

Ant and Honey Bee dragged themselves up the steps, one, two, three, to Cricket's front door. Ant was not going *Blub, blub.* Honey Bee was not going *Buzzzz.*

Cricket opened the door. "No gardeners this year?"

"No," said Ant.

"No," said Honey Bee.

"So what are you?" Cricket asked.

Ant looked at Honey Bee.
Honey Bee looked at Ant.

Maybe Honey Bee's soggy cardboard
lump did not look so lumpy.
Maybe Ant's soggy cardboard blob did
not look so blobby.

"She's a … BEEHIVE!" said Ant.
Honey Bee smiled. "And she's an … ANTHILL!"

"Great idea!" said Cricket. "What a pair!"